Copyright © 1986 Victoria House Publishing Ltd.
First published in Great Britain 1987 by Blackie and Son Ltd.

British Library Cataloguing in Publication Data

Cartwright, Stephen
Such a mess! —— (Blackie first storybooks)
I. Title
823'.914 [J]   PZ7
ISBN 0-216-92195-3

Blackie and Son Ltd.
7 Leicester Place,
London WC2H 7BP

Printed in Singapore

Such a Mess!

Illustrated by Stephen Cartwright
Written by Jean Kenward

Blackie

I wake up early. It is raining. Rain has come in my window. There is a pool of water on the window-sill. I put my teddy in it. Swish . . . swish . . .

'Such a mess!' says Mummy.

We go into the kitchen. Kitty is waiting to be let out. She has torn her cushion with her claws. All the feathers have come out.

'Such a mess!' Mummy says. She brushes
the feathers into a dustpan.
'Atchoo!'
They make her sneeze.

I am having cereal for breakfast today. The cereal tastes funny. There is a feather in it. One, two, three feathers.

Mummy has to tip it out for the birds.
'Such a mess!' she says.

Daddy is late coming downstairs.
'Where is my newspaper?' he asks.

I can see the newspaper. Puppy has it.
What a mess!

Mummy gives me some scrambled eggs.
I have my own spoon. I push my spoon
round and round.

I make the bowl go round and round too.
What fun!

The bowl won't stop.
It falls on the floor.
Crash!

There is yellow and white all over the floor. It makes a funny pattern. 'Such a mess!' sighs Mummy.

Mummy brings a cup of orange juice to the table
and slips on the egg. She tips over the jug.
The juice makes a nice pool.
I put my teddy in it. Swish . . . swish . . .

'Goodbye!' calls Daddy. He is off to work.
'Goodbye!' says Mummy, wiping the table.
'Such a mess!'